Chasing **Tornadoes**

Michael McGuffee
Kelly Burley

Contents

Tornado Alley 4

Thunderstorms. 6

Chasing the Storm 10

Tornado on the Ground!. 14

Clocking the Wind 20

After the Storm. 23

Glossary 24

Rigby

A storm siren screams. People scramble for shelter. A **tornado** is on the ground.

Two white trucks race behind the storm. From each truck, scientists take aim. They point their powerful **radar** dishes at the center of the storm.

The scientists
are about to
clock the fastest
wind speed
ever recorded
on Earth!

Tornado Alley

May 3, 1999

8:00 a.m.

The scientists from the weather lab at Oklahoma University begin this day just like any other spring day, studying weather forecasts. They use maps and computer programs to help them predict tornadoes. The scientists think this is going to be a stormy day in **Tornado Alley.**

Oklahoma University is in an area of the United States called Tornado Alley. More tornadoes occur in this area than in any other part of the world.

Tornado Alley

"Ask the Scientist"

Q: How did you get interested in studying tornadoes?

A: When I was 6 years old, we had a tornado pass within 6 miles of our home. Afterward my father took my family past some of the damage. I was amazed at the power of the tornado and the destruction it caused.

Thunderstorms

10:00 a.m.

South winds are carrying warm, moist air up from the Gulf of Mexico. High in the atmosphere, west winds are carrying cold, dry air down from the Rocky Mountains. When warm, moist air meets cold, dry air, it often causes **thunderstorms.**

Rockies

Gulf of Mexico

Thunderstorms are made of clouds that stretch high above Earth. A tornado develops in about 1 out of 100 thunderstorms.

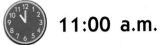 **11:00 a.m.**

After studying the weather maps, the scientists decide conditions are right to produce a type of thunderstorm called a **supercell**. They know that tornadoes often come from supercells.

Characteristics of Supercell Thunderstorms

Strong **updrafts** (vertical winds with speeds up to 120 MPH)

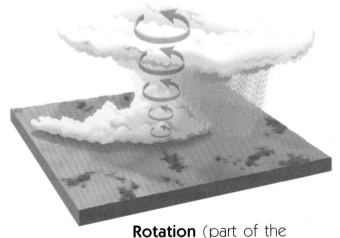

Rotation (part of the thunderstorm is spinning)

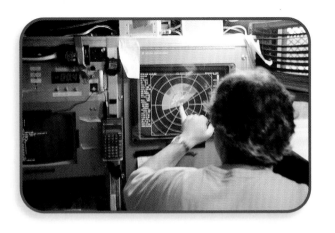

Now the scientists have to predict where and when the **supercell thunderstorms** might happen. The scientists think they will develop late in the afternoon, in southwest Oklahoma. If their prediction is correct, the scientists want to be there in case a tornado forms.

"Ask the Scientist"

Q: How many tornadoes have you seen?

A: In my 13 years of chasing tornadoes, I have seen close to 100 tornadoes, from small "ropes" to mile-wide giants. Some years we see very few, while other years we see many. In one year, I saw 20 tornadoes.

Chasing the Storm

The scientists begin preparing two trucks called Doppler on Wheels. **Doppler** is a special kind of radar that can show if part of a thunderstorm is rotating. The trucks also have radar that shows rain and hail.

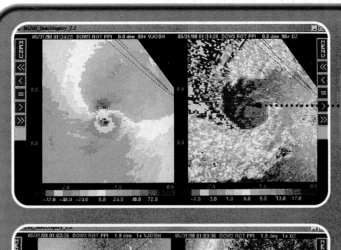

Red areas on radar show heavy rain and hail.

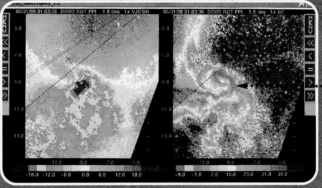

Two colors on Doppler show a thunderstorm that is rotating.

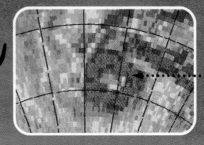

Red "donut" on radar shows a tornado.

11

1:00 p.m.

Two trucks depart from the weather lab. Inside each truck is a driver, a navigator, and a radar operator. The navigator guides the driver. The radar operator studies the storm.

The scientists drive 90 miles before they see their target. A large thunderstorm lies ahead. Radar shows that it has heavy rain and hail.

Tornado on the Ground!

4:45 p.m.

The drivers move into position so that the thunderstorm will go between the two trucks. Doppler radar shows part of the thunderstorm is beginning to rotate. The thunderstorm is becoming a supercell.

5:15 p.m.

A low cloud spins near the back of the supercell. Suddenly, objects begin flying into the air. A tornado is on the ground!

"Ask the Scientist"

Q: How close have you ever been to a tornado?

A: One time we had a weak tornado pass right over our radar truck. It was very brief, but very exciting. Later that same day, we had a tornado form in a field right beside us. That tornado had winds of at least 115 mph. The bigger the tornado is, the farther away we have to stay for safety.

The tornado ends as quickly as it develops. On a scale from 0 to 5, the scientists rank this tornado at 0. Most tornadoes are ranked at 0 or 1.

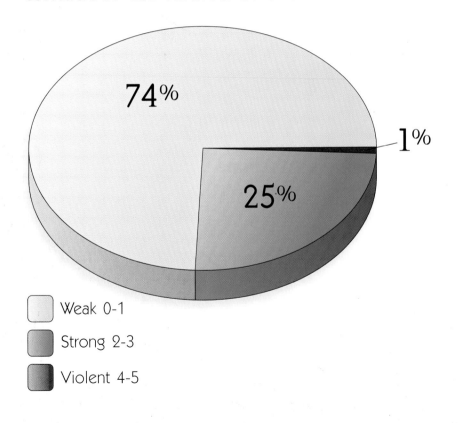

74%

1%

25%

Weak 0-1

Strong 2-3

Violent 4-5

Scale of Tornado Wind Damage

Rank	Wind speed	What the wind can do
0	40-72 mph	break branches on trees
1	73-112 mph	push moving cars off roads
2	113-157 mph	uproot large trees
3	158-206 mph	overturn trains
4	207-260 mph	throw cars in the air
5	261-318 mph	throw car-sized objects more than 100 yards

5:50 p.m.

The scientists believe the supercell will produce another tornado. They quickly move their trucks to a new position. As they race for position, another tornado forms. This tornado is much bigger than the first.

The scientists get a quick reading. The supercell grows bigger and bigger. As the supercell grows, so does the tornado. The scientists are amazed.

"Ask the Scientist"

Q: Is it scary being so close to a tornado?

A: I am usually not scared because we are careful and know what we are doing. However, sometimes it is scary to be in the path of a large, powerful tornado, knowing that if we make a mistake we could be in danger. It is also scary if we are close to a tornado at night when we can't see it.

Clocking the Wind

7:10 p.m.

Now the tornado is nearly a mile wide. Huge objects fly through the air. The scientists stay a safe distance behind the tornado.

The wind roars as they set up for another reading. They clock the fierce wind at 318 miles per hour! It is the fastest wind speed ever recorded!

The scientists
feel both excited
and sad. They have
just recorded the
most violent winds
on the planet.
They have gathered
information that
might one day
help save lives.
But they have also
witnessed the
storm's terrible
destruction.

After the Storm

May 4, 1999

The day after a big storm is always busy at the weather lab as the scientists begin to study their information. This day will be busier than most because the May 3rd tornado was larger and stayed on the ground longer than most of the tornadoes that have been studied.

The information collected from this storm will be used to help scientists understand more about how to predict tornadoes. The scientists know that better predictions will give people more time to seek shelter from nature's most powerful winds.

Glossary

Doppler radar a special kind of radar that measures speed and can show if part of a thunderstorm is rotating

radar a system that uses radio waves to detect certain things, such as rain and hail

rotation the act of turning or spinning

supercell a thunderstorm with strong winds blowing upward as part of the storm spins

thunderstorm a storm with lightning and thunder

tornado a violent, destructive wind with a funnel-shaped cloud that moves in a narrow path across land

Tornado Alley a section of Texas, Oklahoma, and Kansas that has more tornadoes than any other part of the world

updrafts winds blowing up into the sky